The White Curtain

The White Curtain

If ever you have envied a kite, a sailboat or a seagull sailing on a breeze, you'll instantly relate to this magical tale of a curtain with a bad case of wanderlust.

Library of Congress Cataloging-in-Publication Data

Birchmore, Daniel A., 1951-

The White Curtain / written by Daniel A. Birchmore;
illustrated by Gail Lucas
p. cm.

Summary: When a very fine curtain trapped behind a closed window finally finds freedom,
it shares wonderful adventures with a group of happy children before being returned home.

ISBN 1-887813-09-8 (book only: alk. paper)
ISBN 1-887813-11-X (book & audio: alk. paper)

[1. Drapery – Fiction.   2. Adventure and adventurers – Fiction.]
I. Lucas, Gail, 1937- ill.   II. Title.

PZ7.B51179Wh   1996
[E] – dc20

96-7762
CIP AC

Layout and Design by Becca Hutchinson

David C. Lock, Publisher

Printed and bound in Korea by Sung In Printing America, Inc.

Published in the United States by Cucumber Island Storytellers
P.O. Box 920
Montchanin, DE 19710

Please visit our site on the World Wide Web.
http://www.cucumberisland.com

The White Curtain

Written by Daniel A. Birchmore

Illustrated by Gail Lucas

Montchanin, Delaware

Once upon a time there was a pretty white curtain.
It stood nearby a window in the house of a fine lady.

Very often the lady would invite her fine friends over for a fine tea and dine with the fine china on her fine mahogany table.

And her friends would often remark what a fine curtain it was.

One day the wind happened to blow the edge of that fine curtain out the window and what an amazing sight it saw:

bumblebees and butterflies and flowers and trees!
Oh, what a beautiful sight!

The curtain longed to go outside.

The next day a stronger wind blew, and the curtain leaned as far out the window as it could, and suddenly it was free!

It flew with the wind, flapping its sides like a bird
and sailing with the butterflies over the yard

until it landed in a puddle.

It was a nice warm puddle with dark brown water.

The curtain immersed itself in the puddle and soaked luxuriantly in the warm afternoon sun.

Then the fine lady found that her fine curtain was missing and sent everyone in search of it.

"Oh, dear!" she cried when she found her fine white curtain all wet and brown.

So they scrubbed and they scrubbed the curtain until it was all shiny white again and then they put it in its place nearby the window.

And again all the fine ladies who came often for a fine tea remarked how fine a white curtain it was.

But the curtain longed to go outside again, and whenever the wind blew it would peek around the corner of the window to see what was out there.

Then one day a stronger wind blew and the curtain leaned as far out into the wind as it could, and then suddenly it was free!

It flew like a sail as high and as far as it could until it landed in the top of a tree. From the top of that tree the curtain flapped in the breeze like a flag and waved at all the people in the park below.

And from that tree the curtain could see rivers and valleys and hills beyond,

and a lake where white sailboats were skimming across the water. "Oh, what fun that must be to sail over the waters with the winds!" thought the curtain.

Then some children saw the curtain in the tree and said, "Let's make a sailboat!" And so they did.

They brought the curtain home with them and carefully they fastened it to the mast of a small boat and away they sailed!

The white curtain spread itself proudly, holding the wind in its chest, and making the little boat fly across the water!

Every day the curtain and the children would sail across the lake. Then they would fish or swim for awhile, and finally go home for supper.

The curtain would stay awake all night long;

it couldn't wait for the children to return the next morning so they could go sailing!

Then Autumn came and the children had to fold the curtain and put it away for the winter, but when their mother saw the fine white curtain she exclaimed, "Let's use it for a tablecloth!"

And so they did.

And every morning and every evening they carefully set their bowls and their spoons on the pretty white curtain and shared their meal. And the curtain couldn't wait to hear the stories and adventures the children had to tell.

But then one day the family had to move, and they had to leave behind the fine white curtain, and it was sold.

And the fine lady found it in a fine store and bought it

and hung it again in its old place by the fine mahogany table.

And all her fine friends remarked again what a fine curtain it was.

And the curtain was happy to be home again and yet, whenever the sun shone it longed to be outside in the sunshine again, playing with the wind or sailing on the lake.

And one day when the wind was blowing briskly and the sun was shining brightly, it peeked around the corner, saw that no one was watching,

and leaned as far as it could out into the wind...

$15.95

DATE			